PRAISE FOR
MORGAN'S JOURNEY

Morgan's Journey is a promising debut YA novel from Molly Johnston. It is the thought-provoking story of Morgan, who, as the new girl in the neighborhood, is bullied. As she struggles to resolve her conflict, she seeks spiritual guidance from Scripture and her mother. Johnston's story provides life lessons for youth and adults alike.

—Dr. Tom Whalen
Professor of Business,
Massachusetts College of Liberal Arts

Morgan's Journey

Morgan's Journey

Molly Johnston

AUTHOR ACADEMY elite

Published by Author Academy Elite
PO Box 43, Powell, OH 43065
www.AuthorAcademyElite.com

Identifiers:
LCCN: 2021923038
ISBN: 978-1-64746-959-7 (paperback)
ISBN: 978-1-64746-960-3 (hardback)
ISBN: 978-1-64746-961-0 (ebook)

Available in paperback, hardback, e-book, and audiobook

Illustrations by Mairys Jasel

DEDICATION

For Bill, my loving and supportive husband. Thank you for being there for me and always inspiring me to do the best I can and to never give up. You are my strength and my rock, and I love you dearly.

TABLE OF CONTENTS

Dedication vii

Chapter 1   Her Journey Begins 1

Chapter 2   Dream and Play 8

Chapter 3   The Encounter. 12

Chapter 4   The Bike Ride Home 15

Chapter 5   Madison and Morgan. 19

Chapter 6   Lori's Visit 25

Chapter 7   The Birthday Party 28

Chapter 8   The Talk 35

Chapter 9   The Trick. 39

Chapter 10 The Confrontation 48

Chapter 11 Journey's End. 54

Discussion Questions 57

About the Author 59

1

HER JOURNEY BEGINS

Morgan woke to bright sunshine and a summer breeze drifting through the window, swaying the curtains back and forth. She sat up in bed and took a deep breath. Fresh air with the nearby salty ocean made her smile. Her family just moved to Kent Cove, and she already loved it. She couldn't wait to check out the neighborhood and the park with a pond in a wooded area down the street.

Hopeful and excited at the possibility of making new friends, Morgan jumped out of bed and ran down the stairs. Her parents' voices led her to the kitchen, where she found her mom cooking and her dad unpacking a box of plates and platters.

"Good morning," said Morgan.

"Well, look who's finally up." Her mom glanced at Morgan as she entered.

"Good morning. Are you hungry?" her dad added.

"Yup."

"I'm cooking scrambled eggs and bacon, and there's toast on the counter," her mom said, waving a spatula toward the plate filled with perfectly toasted bread.

Morgan eagerly sat at the counter, and her mom placed a glass of orange juice in front of her. She reached for a piece of toast, only to have Dad tease her by pulling the plate just out of reach before pushing it back toward her. She quickly reached for it again, and just as quickly, Dad pulled the plate away. Finally, on the third try, she snagged a piece.

"Ha!" she shouted, waving the toast in victory.

Dad laughed and put an arm around her shoulder to give her a hug. "Okay, okay. You win."

"All right, you two here's breakfast," Mom said, placing a platter in front of them. "Please don't sling it on the floor."

"We wouldn't think of playing with food this good," Dad said, giving Morgan a wink as he reached for a spoon to scoop some eggs onto his plate.

Morgan put eggs onto her toast, topped it with crispy bacon, and folded the toast in half. It was her own crunchy breakfast creation.

"No way!" she agreed, just before taking a big bite.

"Take it easy, Kiddo; don't choke," Dad said while watching Morgan gulp down her food.

Mom rolled her eyes at both of them. "Uh-huh," she said as she began filling a plate for herself.

Morgan's breakfast was gone in a couple of bites. Swiping the crumbs from her face with her arm, she hopped off the stool. "Can I go outside? I want to explore the neighborhood."

"Sure," her mom said. "Just pay attention to where you are and don't go too far."

Morgan dashed upstairs to change out of pajamas and into a pair of jeans, a red t-shirt, and black sneakers. She went to the bathroom to brush her hair into a ponytail, brushed her teeth, and hurried back downstairs to poke her head back into the kitchen. "I'll see you guys later."

"Be careful, honey," Mom said.

"I will be."

Morgan hurried through the door to the garage, slamming it shut behind her as she pushed the button to open the outer garage door. It creaked and groaned and rattled its way up the tracks. *What a racket*, she thought as she put her helmet on and walked her bike outside. *Wow, what a beautiful day.*

She climbed on her pink and purple Huffy bike with streamers dangling from the handlebars and sailed down the driveway. Her neighbors on both sides of the street were out in their yards, mowing their lawns or planting flowers to welcome summer. At the end of the road, she turned around and headed back toward her house. As she got closer to her next-door neighbor, she saw a girl practicing her hoop shots. She slowed her bike to a stop at the edge of the girl's driveway and put her foot down to keep herself steady.

The girl, who looked about Morgan's age, gave her a half-smile while asking, "You just moved in yesterday, right?"

"Yeah. You're pretty good at that," Morgan said, nodding at the ball. "I'm Morgan. What's your name?"

"I'm Madison. Where did—"

Before she could finish, another girl hollered at Morgan as she jogged from across the street.

"Who are you?"

"I'm Morgan."

The girl looked Morgan over and smirked. "I'm not sure if I like you."

Morgan's mouth fell open. "Why? You don't even know me."

"Doesn't matter. You're not Katie. I was best friends with her," the girl said as she grabbed the ball from Madison.

"I think it does matter," Morgan said matter-of-factly. "How can you know if you don't like me if you don't take the time to get to know me?" She gripped the handlebars as she spoke, knuckles turning white.

"Are you done? Do you really have to go on like that?" Lori said in disgust.

Embarrassed, Morgan straightened her ponytail and said, "Sorry, I'm trying to be nice."

"Don't try. I don't care who you are, and I don't need you to be nice to me."

"So, don't tell me your name. I thought it would be a good idea to know who my neighbor is," said Morgan.

"Fine. My name is Lori, and I live across the street in the red house. Happy now?"

"Yes, thank you."

Lori turned her back as she tossed the ball back to Madison, saying, "You can't talk to her until I decide if I want her to be a part of our group." Then, looking hard again at Morgan, she made a point of rolling her eyes in disgust before heading back across the street.

Madison tossed the ball up into the air. As it came down, she said, "Lori kinda *runs* the neighborhood."

"What do you mean, she 'kinda *runs* the neighborhood?'"

"It's simple. If you're friends with Lori, she expects you to do what she says and follow her rules. If you don't do what she says to do, you can't be in the group," said Madison.

"What group?" Morgan asked. "And why does she get to decide who can be friends?"

"Well, that's how it is with Lori. Either you're in or not. And she'll make sure you know you're not. Anyway, I better go before she sees me still talking to you," said Madison, as she nervously moved her body from one foot to the other.

"Well, bye, I guess," Morgan said.

"Yeah, bye."

Dazed by the crazy conversation, Morgan watched the girl walk away from her. "What just happened? Well, nobody's going to tell me who I can be friends with," she said to no one. Shaking her head, she pushed her bike into motion again and headed toward the other end of the road.

At the end of the street, she came to a wooded area with a pond encircled by a path. There was a small park with swings, monkey bars, and a slide with a fort attached to it. Morgan got off her bike and let it fall to the ground so she could explore the area.

She walked to the swings first and swung for a while, stretching her feet to see how high she could reach. Then she leaped from the swing, landing almost perfectly, and went to check out the pond. As she watched the ducks preening at the water's edge, she heard laughter in the distance and turned her head to see Lori, Madison, and four other girls riding their bikes into the park and Lori jabbing a finger in her direction.

The girls rode to where Morgan sat and made a semi-circle around her with their bikes. "What are you doing here?" Lori asked.

"I'm checking out the pond," Morgan said.

"Well, you can't sit here because this is where we come to talk about things, and you're not a friend. Get lost!" said Lori.

Morgan just looked at her and said, "I can sit here. You can't tell me what to do."

The girls laughed.

Lori responded, "Yes, I can tell you what to do. Get lost, or I'll make you go for a swim."

Morgan didn't want any trouble and got up to walk away.

"Don't come here again, loser," snickered Lori.

As Morgan walked past them, Madison made a face at her, and the girls laughed again as she got on her bike and hurried home.

Morgan entered the house to find her mom and dad in the family room, taking photos out of a box to hang on the wall.

"Hey, honey, back so soon?" said her mom.

"Yeah."

"Did you see anything exciting on your adventure?" asked her dad.

"Nothing too exciting. Met some of the girls who live in the neighborhood."

"Who is the girl who lives next door?" he asked.

"Oh, that's Madison."

"Is she nice?" Her mom held a picture up, eyeing where she thought it would fit.

"She's okay, I guess."

"You don't seem as excited as you were when you got up this morning. Are you sure everything's okay?"

"Yeah, everything's okay. Dad, you're a lawyer. So, what's bullying?"

"Well, it's mostly when a person deliberately hurts someone else to get attention, be popular, or even just be in control. When someone picks on others, they feel big and important.

"Bullies might come from families full of strife or are around angry people who yell a lot, and they think it's okay to act that way. It's learned behavior. Some bullies know they're hurting people, but some don't realize their actions are hurting someone else. Did that information help?"

"Yes, that helped. Suppose someone was being bullied. Is it okay to stand up to the bully?" Morgan asked.

"Of course. It's okay to stand up to someone, but it's not okay to hurt them or call them names. Sometimes it's best to walk away and not give them a chance to hurt you or continue to say mean things. Not saying anything might be the best weapon you can use against someone."

"Were the girls mean to you, Morgan?" asked her mom.

"No."

Morgan knew she wasn't being honest with her parents, but she didn't want them to know what happened. She left, heading to the patio to sit by the pool.

For the rest of the day, Morgan didn't say much to anyone. She kept thinking about what Lori said to her and how the girls treated her, including Madison.

Maybe what she said about Lori was true.

Morgan remained quiet during dinner and didn't want to watch television with her parents. She even passed up her mom's offer of popcorn. Instead, she went to her room to read a book and be alone.

2

DREAM AND PLAY

Later that evening, Morgan's mom knocked on her bedroom door.

"Yeah," said Morgan.

"Are you okay?" She slowly opened Morgan's door to peek inside.

"What do you want?"

"Just checking in on you. We missed spending time with you watching television and eating popcorn."

"I'm fine, okay? Leave me alone!"

"Morgan, your tone of voice is not kind. Do you want to talk about something?"

Morgan changed her tone, took a deep breath, and said, "I'm sorry, Mom. No, I don't want to talk. I'm okay, really."

"Okay. If you need anything, you know where to find me."

"Sure."

"Alright, good night." Her mom closed the door.

Morgan grabbed her pillow and Mr. Binks the Bear and then lay down at the foot of her bed, sobbing into the pillow and holding the bear close to her. Her pain was too much, but she couldn't talk to her mom. At least, not yet.

After a good long cry, sleepiness came over her. She got up to put on her pajamas, wiping her tears away with the back of her hand. Morgan brushed her teeth, washed her face, and then went to bed. She had a tough time getting to sleep. She tossed and turned for ages, and when she finally fell asleep, she had a bad dream about walking by herself down a dark path in the woods.

Then, a loud clang of metal hitting metal startled Morgan from a sound sleep. Still half asleep, she sat up in bed as a horrible stench of rotting food and diesel floated in through the open window. Pinching her nose closed, she mumbled, "My God, what is that disgusting smell?" She stumbled out of bed and looked outside. Slamming the window shut, she noticed men throwing garbage into the back of a garbage truck. It drove away, exposing Lori and Madison talking in Lori's driveway. Morgan started to walk away when she saw Lori look up and point a finger at her window with an offended look on her face. Madison turned around to catch Morgan watching them.

Embarrassed, she quickly turned away from the window, "Oh, darn. They saw me. Now, they probably think I'm spying on them." Giggling, she said, "Morgan, the spy," and went over to her bed to straighten the sheets and put her pillows against the headboard. She picked up Mr. Binks from the floor and plopped him in the middle of the bed.

She walked to her door, letting it swing open, and headed downstairs. In the kitchen, she poured herself a glass of orange juice, then put some fruity-flavored cereal into a bowl with milk, and carried her breakfast to the kitchen island to sit down. She saw a note from her mom explaining she went to the grocery store and would be home soon. While Morgan ate, she noticed the iPod she'd left on the island and finished the game she started the other day. When she finished eating, she put her bowl and glass in the dishwasher and put the milk and juice away.

Morgan went upstairs to get dressed and brush her teeth and hair. While in the bathroom, she looked at herself in the mirror and was perfectly happy with what she saw. She was confident in herself and decided she would make the best of what had happened yesterday. "Who cares if they don't like me? I can't change who they are," she said out loud. The one thing that bothered her was the dream from the other night. "Where is the path, and why did I dream about it? Oh, well. I can't let a silly dream get to me." So, she put the thought behind her and rushed down to the garage, put on her helmet, and got on her bike. Her mom left the garage door open, so she rode her bike right out of the garage and down the driveway.

As Morgan rode past Lori's house, looking up, she saw Lori and Madison watching her from Lori's bedroom window. She continued to ride down the road toward the park.

Morgan saw the swings and decided to stop. She got off her bike and let it fall to the ground before walking to the middle swing. She pushed her feet off the ground and started pumping her legs back and forth to go faster and higher. Up and up, she went like a bird flying through the sky. Morgan closed her eyes and let her head fall back, her long brown hair trailing behind her as she allowed the momentum of the swing to carry her through the air. The swing slowed, and she brought her head upright, opening her eyes. She could hear voices in the distance, creating an uneasiness inside her.

3

THE ENCOUNTER

Morgan looked down the road; nervousness stirred inside her when she saw Lori and the girls riding their bikes toward the swings. They stopped near the swings, and Lori got off her bike, swinging her arms with purpose as she walked toward Morgan. Lori and Morgan never broke eye contact. Morgan didn't want Lori to know

she was quivering inside; she prayed to God, asking for the strength to help her get through the encounter. She knew Lori was up to no good, so she kept reminding herself to stay calm and not fight with her.

Lori sat on the swing next to her. She motioned one of the girls to sit on the other side of Morgan and the rest to stand in front of her, blocking her from leaving. Lori jabbed her finger into Morgan's arm and said, "Watching me from your window, huh? Don't you ever watch me again! If I catch you doing it, I'll beat you up," Lori angrily said to Morgan.

"Go ahead and beat me up. What are you afraid of?" Said Morgan.

"I'm not afraid of you. And another thing. I told you yesterday the park is off-limits to you."

"You said you don't want me sitting at the pond. I thought taking a swing today wouldn't be a problem."

"You thought wrong!"

"I don't understand. I don't see your name on the park, so you don't have the right to tell me not to play here."

Lori pursed her lips and crinkled her eyebrows. "You are worthless and stupid," she said as her friends laughed.

Morgan stood up, but the girls moved forward, forcing her to sit back down on the swing.

"Ha, you're outnumbered. What are you going to do about it?"

"I'm going to do this." Standing up, Morgan kicked one of the girls in the leg and pushed her way through them. She ran to her bike, but before she could get on it, Lori caught up with her, grabbed her arm, and pulled her back.

"Thought you could get away? Stupid move."

"Let me go home, and I won't come here again, I promise."

Lori smirked. "You think I'm that stupid to let you go? Well, do you?"

Morgan said nothing.

Using both hands, Lori shoved Morgan in the chest, causing her to stumble over a rock and fall. Her head hit the ground, and she was thankful she still had her bike helmet on. She looked up and saw the girls rushing to keep her from getting up. Morgan wrapped her arms around her head to protect it.

"What's the matter, Morgan? Are you afraid we're gonna hurt you?" Lori said with a mocking tone.

Morgan sat up and pulled her arms away from her head. Then she looked at Lori and said, "You know you'll never get away with bullying me."

"Ha! Do you see anyone stopping me?"

"Why do you want to hurt me?"

Lori kneeled on the ground next to her. "You're not our friend, and I don't like you." Getting up, she stood over Morgan with her arms crossed and hate in her eyes.

Morgan tried to get up, but the girls pushed her back down. Pleased with themselves, they high-fived each other.

"You are such a nobody. No one in this neighborhood will ever like you," Lori grinned.

Morgan quickly rolled toward her, grabbed her leg, and pulled, causing Lori to lose her balance. She staggered, tripping over one of the bikes. While the girls helped her up, Morgan jumped on her bike and rode away.

"She's getting away!" one of the girls called out.

They rushed to their bikes to go after Morgan, but Madison blocked Lori with her bike. Putting her feet on the ground to keep herself steady, Lori yelled at the rest of the girls, "Go after her! Don't let her get away! Madison, get out of my way!"

"What are we doing, Lori?" Madison asked with concern in her voice.

"I'm going after her because no one makes a fool out of me and gets away with it."

"A fool? She was protecting herself. Don't hurt her."

"Protecting herself? She deserves everything she gets."

"Lori, you need to stop."

With viciousness in her eyes, Lori said, "I can make your life miserable. Get out of my way!"

Scared, Madison backed up and let Lori go by.

4

THE BIKE RIDE HOME

Morgan peddled so fast her knees were practically hitting her chest. She could see a long hill up ahead and wondered if she could even make it home before the girls caught up to her. It was fun going down, coasting without peddling, but it was tough going up, and she dreaded the upcoming climb. She heard a noise behind her and turned her head to see the girls and Lori pumping hard to catch her. Morgan quickly turned back around just as she almost ran off the road. She corrected her path and started to climb the hill. Halfway up, she grew tired and slowed down. Her breathing grew heavy, and sweat ran down the side of her face. *Come on, Morgan, you can do it.*

Lori kept calling her name, taunting her, "Morgan . . . , Morgan . . ."

She peddled faster and never looked back but then looked to her left and saw Lori coming up next to her. *Oh, great.*

Panting and trying to catch her breath between words, Lori asked, "Having a tough time with the hill?"

"Leave me alone."

"Oh, come on. That's not nice."

Winded, Morgan said, "You are the last to talk about being nice."

They made it to the crest of the hill, and she could see their neighborhood. Riding side by side as they descended the hill, Lori slid close to her, trying to get Morgan to go off the road. Missing the first time, Lori tried again. Luckily, Morgan saw it coming and hit her brakes. Lori went flying past her.

"Darn!" Lori quickly turned her bike and hurried back. As soon as Lori got close, Morgan pushed off with her feet and rushed past her, making Lori look like a fool.

Again, Lori swiftly turned around and peddled fast, trying to catch up to her. Morgan saw her house and focused on it, giving her hope she would make it. She was sure Lori wouldn't try anything with neighbors around to catch her. *Come on, come on. A little bit farther, Morgan, and you're home free.*

Lori couldn't keep up. Tired and breathing heavily, she stopped in the road and watched Morgan ride away. She took her fist and hit it against the handlebar, angry she had to give up. The other girls stopped around Lori, trying to catch their breath. Madison watched as Morgan turned into her driveway and disappeared into the garage. She smiled to herself secretly. She was happy Morgan had made it home safely.

One of the panting girls finally spoke, "What now?"

"Oh, shut up," said Lori.

The girl shrugged her shoulders and stared down at the road.

"Go home," Lori said as she looked at all of the girls.

They rode away, leaving Lori in the road by herself.

"The next time I see you, Morgan, you will pay for defeating me!" she said under her breath before heading home.

Morgan put her foot down to steady the bike, and the pain from her knee went up and down her leg. She took off her helmet and used the strap to hang it from the handlebar. Wincing, she limped to the button and closed the squeaky, rattling garage door. Morgan opened the door that led from the garage to the mudroom letting it swing open and hit the wall behind it. "Oops. I hope I didn't put a dent in the wall." Morgan said to herself. Shoving the door shut, she hobbled to the bench and sat down, kicking off her sneakers and leaving them in a pile on the floor. When she stood up, her knee cracked loudly. "Dang, that hurts!" Her entire body ached like she had been run over by a freight train. She slowly walked into the kitchen to find her mom at the island, drinking a glass of water and typing away at her laptop. Her Mom looked up from her computer to see Morgan limp across the room to sit next to her.

"Hi, honey. What happened to you?"

"I fell off my bike," said Morgan. Lying to her mom was wrong and would get her in trouble, but she couldn't tell her what really happened with Lori.

"How?"

"Came down the hill too fast. I need some water and aspirin, please."

"Sure, I'll get it for you."

"Thank you, Mom." She took the aspirin and drank the entire glass of water; it was refreshing after a difficult experience.

"Not a problem. Are you alright?"

"Yeah, just sore. After a hot shower and rest, I'll be okay."

"Your dad will be home late tonight. Pizza, okay?"

"Sounds good."

Morgan slowly went upstairs to take a shower. Every step hurt.

5

MADISON AND MORGAN

The next day, Madison went to Morgan's house to see if she was okay. She rang the front doorbell, and Morgan's mom answered the door.

"Hi, Mrs. Jones, I'm Madison from next door. How is Morgan doing?"

She crinkled her eyebrows and replied, "Hi Madison. I guess she's doing okay. Excuse me for asking, but why are you wondering how she is?" asked Morgan's mom.

"I was with her yesterday."

"You were?"

"Yes, I went to the park, and when I got there, she was on a swing. So, I joined her. We swung for a while and then raced each other home on our bikes."

"Is that how she fell off her bike?"

"Um, yes."

Morgan's mom tilted her head and gave Madison a smile that made it clear she knew she wasn't getting the whole truth. "Where are my manners? Please come in."

"Thank you," Madison said as she entered the house.

"I'll go get her. She's upstairs in her room. Please have a seat at the island."

On her way there, Madison looked around, remembering the fun times she had with Katie when she lived here. She sat at the island and waited patiently. A few minutes later, Morgan walked in as her mom followed.

"Here she is, Madison, a little tired and sore. I made an apple pie this morning. Care to have a piece?"

"Yes, please. Apple pie is my favorite," she grinned.

"Morgan, can I get you a piece too?"

"Yes, thank you, Mom."

Delighted the girls wanted some pie, she cut two pieces and took plates from the cupboard. "I didn't know Madison was with you yesterday, Morgan."

"Oh, I forgot to mention that."

Turning from the counter, she placed the plates in front of the girls and said, "I guess you did. It's still warm; I wish I had some ice cream to put on top. Enjoy! I'll leave you two girls to talk."

"Thank you," said Madison.

"You're welcome and nice to meet you, Madison."

The girls waited until Morgan's mom left the kitchen before they started to talk.

Madison picked up her plate and held it right under her nose. "*Mmmm*, I love the smell of apple pie." She set her plate on the counter and began wolfing it down. With her mouth full, she said, "Oh my gosh, so yummy!"

Morgan laughed at her and said, "You really love that pie."

Smiling, Madison's head bobbed up and down.

"Will you stop eating long enough to talk?"

Madison swallowed her mouthful and asked, "What do you want to talk about?"

"Why are you here?"

"Yesterday was bad. I thought Lori was tough on you, but it was cool you held your own."

"What's up with her?"

Madison moved the pie around with her fork. "I don't know what's up with her. I tried to stop her when she got on her bike to go after you. She threatened me, and I . . . was scared of her." She put the bite in her mouth and pushed her plate away. "I don't remember her being a bully before Katie moved. Katie, she, and I were like the three musketeers."

"Wow, thanks for trying to stop her. Who's Katie?"

"Katie lived in this house before you."

"Tell me more about Katie."

"Like I said, three musketeers. Ya know, good friends. We did everything together. But then she moved to California, and Lori changed. She's angry a lot."

"Why did Katie move to California?"

"Her dad was transferred. They had to leave because of his job."

"We moved here because my dad became a partner at the law firm in town."

"Oh. That's why you moved here?"

Morgan shook her head up and down.

"Has Lori shared with you why she doesn't like me?" said Morgan.

"No. I don't get it. It doesn't make any sense. You seem nice."

"I think I'm nice."

"Lori scares me sometimes. I'm never sure what she'll do," said Madison.

"She scares me too. I'm afraid to go outside now."

"That sucks."

"I know. I love to ride my bike."

"Maybe I can talk with her and find out why she hates you. I like you. I think you're pretty cool!"

"So, you think I'm cool?"

"Yeah. Why do you think I'm here?"

Morgan shrugged her shoulders and said, "To get me to talk so you can tell Lori. You weren't nice to me yesterday."

"I know. I'm sorry. But I was happy when you made it to your driveway."

"Yeah, so was I. Will you tell her we talked?"

"No way!" She crossed her fingers and said, "I promise!"

Morgan smiled at her and ate her last piece of pie.

"Um, I better go. I hope to see you around."

As the girls hopped off their stools and came around the corner, they saw Mrs. Jones straightening a crooked picture on the wall.

"I'll be seeing you."

"Yup, see ya." Madison walked outside and headed back to her house.

Soon after Madison returned home, there was a knock at the door. She answered it and was surprised to see Lori standing there. *Did she know about my visit with Morgan?* Madison thought to herself.

"Hey, Lori."

"Don't 'Hey, Lori' me," she said as she pushed her way into the house, knocking Madison off balance.

"I saw you at Morgan's house. Why?"

"What do you mean?"

Poking Madison in the chest, she said, "Don't give me that!"

Madison used her hand to block her chest, and Lori moved her finger away. "I was riding my bike up the road when I saw you leave her house."

"Oh."

Lori paced—stomped—back and forth. "We are friends, and she is not. You are not to talk to her," she said, practically yelling.

"Lori, stop! I wanted to make sure she was okay."

"Why do you care if she is okay?"

"You were tough on her yesterday."

Lori stopped pacing and looked at Madison with rage in her eyes. She was suddenly afraid Lori was going to hurt her. Madison's heart beat faster, nearly jumping out of her chest.

Lori yelled, "So what?"

"It's . . . not right!"

Lori shook her finger in Madison's face and exclaimed, "You're really getting on my nerves!"

Madison stepped backward as she said, "Sorry I'm getting on your nerves. I think you should try being nice to her."

Lori laughed, "Seriously? Nice to her?" Moving closer to Madison, she screamed in her face, "Never!"

"She told me she's afraid—"

"Madison?" her mother asked, "Afraid of what, Madison?"

Lori spun around to see Mrs. Roberts standing behind her. Lori looked worried and uncomfortable because she knew she was caught bullying Madison.

She immediately straightened up and smiled. "Hi, Mrs. Roberts."

"*Mm-hmm,*" said Madison's mom as she looked at Lori without smiling back.

"From the commotion out here, I take it you're upset with Madison. Does it happen to have anything to do with our new neighbor?"

"Yes," Lori answered.

"I see. Care to share with me what it is that has you coming into my house and yelling at my daughter?"

"*Umm . . . ,*" Lori fidgeted as tears formed in her eyes.

"I was in my office, and I heard everything you said. The next time you come to talk with Madison, please respect my daughter and be kind to her. God loves it when we can show kindness to each other. Show our new neighbor some kindness, as well, and invite her to your birthday party. Make her feel welcome regardless of how you feel about her; you might end up liking her. With that said, it's time for you to go home."

Looking down at the floor, Lori said, "I'm sorry, Mrs. Roberts. I'll invite Morgan to my party."

"Good. Just remember to be nice to her because it will be better for you in the long run."

Lori nodded, "I'll remember. See ya, Madison. Goodbye, Mrs. Roberts."

"Goodbye, Lori," Madison's mom said as she gently shut the door and returned to her office.

6

LORI'S VISIT

The next morning, Morgan and her mom were outside planting petunias, marigolds, bleeding hearts, and other flowers in the front garden.

"Hello, you must be Lori," Morgan's mom said as she stood up and walked toward the girl approaching them. Morgan jumped to her feet when she heard Lori's name and quickly stepped back, dropping her trowel. Her mom jerked her head upward and gave Morgan a strange and confused look as she spoke to the girl. "What brings you here?"

"Hi, Mrs. Jones. I came over to talk to Morgan."

"Of course. I need some water. Can I get you girls some too?"

"No. Thank you."

Morgan shook her head no. "Mom, you can stay. Whatever Lori has to say, she can say it in front of you."

"Morgan, don't be silly. I'll be in the kitchen." She stopped at the door and took her dirty garden boots off, leaving them on the stoop.

Once she was in the house and closed the door, Lori walked over to Morgan. "Look, I'll just cut to the chase. I'm sorry. What I did yesterday was wrong."

"You're sorry?" Morgan was surprised by her apology, thinking it was another one of her tricks.

"Yeah," she said, rolling her eyes.

Not knowing what else to say, they stood staring at each other. Lori finally looked around and noticed the garden. "These flowers are pretty. You and your mom must have been busy planting."

"Yeah, we like doing that together."

Lori nodded and said, "Well, umm, I guess I'll be going."

"Yup, okay."

Lori walked partway down the driveway before she remembered something. She turned around and saw Morgan heading to the house. "Hey, Morgan?"

She turned around. "What?"

"Umm, my birthday is this Saturday, and I'm having a party. Want to come?"

"You want me to come to your party?"

"Yeah." Lori crossed her arms.

"I'll only go if Madison will be there."

"She will be."

"Will your mom be there?"

"Yeah, of course."

"Okay, I'll go."

"Great. It starts at one."

"I'll see you then."

"See ya."

When Morgan turned around, she saw her mom watching from the kitchen window and was relieved to know she was there. Morgan went inside and kicked her muddy boots off in the foyer before going into the kitchen.

"She seems nice," her mom said.

Morgan smirked to herself, "She's okay."

"What did she want?"

"She invited me to her birthday party this Saturday."

"Oh, that was nice of her. Are you going?"

"Yes."

"Well, we should go shopping for a gift. How about we go after we finish planting the rest of the flowers?"

"Yeah, sure."

They finished with the flowerbed, changed into clean clothes, brushed their teeth and hair, and headed out. Morgan's mom drove them into town to shop at the Card and Candle, where Morgan found cute, purple ladybug earrings and a matching flowery necklace. After her mom paid for the gift, they headed to the Cold Scoop to get ice cream; they sat on a bench by the pier and ate while overlooking the Atlantic Ocean.

7

THE BIRTHDAY PARTY

Morgan was in her room singing along to the radio and dancing as if she were on stage, performing in front of her fans. A commercial came on just as she heard a message chime. Morgan turned off the radio and grabbed her phone from the dresser to see it was from Madison.

"Hey, how are you?"

"Hey, I'm good. What are you doing?"

"I'm getting ready to go to the party."

"When are you going?"

"Around one. We can go together if you want."

"Sounds good!"

"Okay. I'll wait for you outside."

Time was ticking by, and Morgan needed to get ready. She put on white shorts, a flowered top, and brown sandals before pulling her hair back into a ponytail and tying a yellow ribbon around the band. Looking at herself in the full-length mirror, she twirled around and said, "You look good." She laughed at herself and grabbed Lori's gift off the dresser, then went out the door and downstairs to say goodbye to her mom.

She yelled, "Mom, leaving for the party."

"You don't have to yell. I'm right here," she said as she entered the foyer.

"Oh, sorry."

"Well, don't you look nice? Very pretty. Have a good time and remember your manners."

She smiled and rolled her eyes. "I will," she said as she rushed out the front door, letting it slam.

Her Mom winced, "My gosh, I wish she would stop slamming the doors around here!"

As Morgan hurried along the walkway, Madison hurried toward her.

"Hi."

"Hey, Morgan. I like your outfit."

"Thanks, I like yours too." They walked across the street to Lori's house, and Madison rang the doorbell.

While waiting for someone to open the door, Madison asked Morgan if she had ever met Mrs. Fletcher.

"No, not yet."

"She's nice."

"That's—" Before Morgan could finish what she was saying, Mrs. Fletcher opened the door.

"Hi, girls, please come in. The party is on the screened porch."

They thanked her, and Madison led the way out back. Morgan's confidence disappeared when she recognized the same girls from the day Lori bullied her at the park. The noise was overwhelming as the girls talked over each other, but a sudden hush came over the room when they saw Morgan. The feeling in the room grew tense when they started whispering to each other while casting glances in her direction. Morgan heard one of the girls say, "What is she doing here?" The girl shrugged her shoulders.

Morgan immediately thought it might have been a bad idea to come. She hoped Mrs. Fletcher would stay during the party and was relieved when she stepped onto the porch with them.

"Lori, all of your friends are here. Shall we start with some games?" asked Mrs. Fletcher.

"Yeah, let's get started," Lori agreed with her mom.

"Hi, Morgan. Glad you came," Lori said as she walked past Morgan, smiling.

Morgan smiled back at her, "Thanks."

"Girls, can you give me those packages, and I'll put them on the gift table?" said Mrs. Fletcher.

Lori then said, "How about we have a three-legged race? Follow me to the yard." Excited, the girls all started talking at once and rushed down the stairs together. Mrs. Fletcher followed them and stood to the side of the yard.

They cheered each other on and pointed fingers at each other while laughing.

"We're taking you down!" Madison said to the girls as she picked Morgan to be her partner.

Cindy and Anna reacted to Madison, "Oh, no, we're going to win!"

Lori didn't have a partner but helped the girls tie their legs together with pieces of cloth cut into long strips. Once everyone was ready, she said, "On your mark, get set, go!"

Morgan noticed two of the girls kept falling and struggled to get up. Madison and Morgan were doing great, but Cindy and Anna passed them and won. Madison and Morgan came in second. Third place went to the girls who kept falling. They became the laughingstock of the party; so much so, they laughed at themselves. Even Mrs. Fletcher couldn't stop laughing. Lori helped them get up and untied the cloth from their legs.

"Thanks, Lori," said one of the girls who was on the ground.

"No, prob," said Lori.

Everything was going great. Morgan was having fun and was happy she came to the party because Lori was being nice to her.

Lori said, "How about we break open the piñata?"

Everyone cried out, "Yeah!"

"Who wants to go first?" Lori asked as they gathered by the tree in the corner of the yard where the piñata hung from a low branch.

"I do," said one of the girls.

Lori tied a black ribbon around her head, covering her eyes. She spun the girl around three times, handed her a baseball bat, and faced her toward the piñata. After the girl swung and missed, the girls tried to tell her where to hit it. But it didn't help.

Morgan periodically watched Lori's mom to make sure she was still in the yard. She became concerned when Mrs. Fletcher's phone rang, and she left the yard to take the call.

Lori said, "Okay, time to give you a break and let someone else try. Morgan, it's your turn." Smiling, she grabbed Morgan's arm and walked her closer to the piñata.

"I'm good. That girl wanted to do it. Let her," said Morgan.

"Oh, no, it's your turn."

Lori tied the cloth around Morgan's head, covering her eyes, and Morgan immediately got a bad feeling in her stomach.

"Wait, I want to do it," Madison said.

"No, it's Morgan's turn," Lori said as she pushed Madison away.

Morgan prayed Lori's mom would come back, but she didn't. Lori handed Morgan a baseball bat and spun her around three times, then pushed her.

Morgan lost her balance and fell to the ground. She got up, and Lori took her hand to reposition her near the piñata before spinning her around three times again. Every time Morgan tried to hit the piñata, she missed. The girls laughed at her and called her names. "You are useless. You can't even hit a stupid piñata with a baseball bat."

"Just stop so I can take the cloth off your stupid face," Lori said as she yanked the blindfold off.

Morgan felt brokenhearted and looked to Madison for comfort. She got no response from her. Morgan didn't know what to do; she wanted to go home but thought it would be rude to leave. She was relieved when she saw Mrs. Fletcher walk back into the yard.

"What's going on? I thought I heard some yelling and name-calling," Mrs. Fletcher said.

"Everything is fine, Mom. Just having some fun. No name-calling," Lori replied, suddenly back to being her fake nice self. She then gave the girl who'd wanted a turn before Morgan a try at the piñata. On her third hit, she broke it open. The girls rushed to get the candy that had fallen to the ground, but Morgan wanted nothing to do with it and stayed to the side.

Looking at her watch, Lori's mom said, "Okay, it's time for cupcakes and singing Happy Birthday to Lori. Let's head back to the porch."

The girls giggled as they rushed up the stairs. As they entered the porch, they admired the pretty table decorated with different shades of purple plates and napkins. In the middle of the table sat cookies, candy, and different types of snacks for them to eat. The girls sat at the table, making sure Morgan couldn't sit next to any of them. Morgan took a seat next to Madison, still wishing she could leave. Her shorts had grass stains on them, her pride was hurt, and she wanted to cry.

Lori passed out the cupcakes, and then she sat down at the table. They sang "Happy Birthday" to her before she blew out the candles on her cupcake. When they finished eating, they watched Lori open her presents. Mrs. Fletcher's phone rang again, and she got up to take the call. Lori grabbed the present from Morgan.

She held Morgan's gift up and announced, "This is from Morgan." She opened it, and when she saw the matching jewelry set, she tossed it on the floor. "Ugly!"

Morgan somehow kept herself from crying; the girls laughed at her. When Lori finished opening the gifts, it was time for everyone to leave. She handed out gift bags for everyone to take home—everyone except Morgan. Madison saw what she did and handed Morgan her gift bag instead. Lori walked past Madison, glared at her as she snagged the gift bag from Morgan's hand, and hurled it into the garbage.

"Come on, Morgan. Let's go," Madison said. They left together, leaving Lori alone to throw her tantrum.

She picked up Morgan's gift from the floor and threw it into the trash as she yelled after them, "I hate you, Morgan!"

The two girls ignored her and walked back to Morgan's house.

"I'm sorry," said Madison.

"Why are you sorry? You didn't do anything."

"Yes and no. My mom told her to invite you to her party hoping she would be nice. I was hoping she would like you."

"It's okay. She's Lori. She was nice when her mom was around."

"Yeah, she was."

"You want to come in?"

"I have to get home. My mom is expecting me."

"Sure, not a problem. See you around?"

Madison smiled weakly, "Yeah."

8

THE TALK

Morgan entered her house. Tears streamed down her face. She stood in the foyer crying.

Her mom called out to her, "Morgan, is that you?" As she approached, she added, "How was the—" She stopped when she saw Morgan sobbing. "Oh, honey," she said, reaching her arms out to hold her. They hugged each other tightly for a long time because Morgan didn't want to stop; she wanted her mom to take her pain away.

When she couldn't cry anymore, she said, "Mom, I'm okay."

She saw the remorse in her mother's eyes as she held Morgan's face in her hands, wiping her tears away with her thumbs. "Come, let us go into the family room and talk about what happened." Leading her by the hand she added, "I can only imagine what Lori did to you."

Morgan's heart was ripped apart, and she wasn't sure if her mom knew how much she was hurting inside. As they sat down on the couch, her mom said, "Tell me what happened."

Morgan swallowed and told her everything. When she was done, she started to cry again. Her mom put her arm around her shoulders and pulled her close, telling her, "Let it all go."

When Morgan had no tears left, she moved away from her mom and looked at her. "Why do people hate?"

"That's a good question. I guess it's because they hurt inside, so sometimes they need to feel in control and get what they want every time. It could also be she is jealous of you. Only Lori has the answer. What angers me is she turned her birthday party into a cruel attack on you. I want to go over there and speak my mind; my head says to do it, but my heart says no. I have to listen to my heart because I feel it's God telling me it would be a bad idea. The timing is not right."

"Then when?"

"Well, if it continues—which I'm sure it will, we will pray to God and ask him for guidance. We should never do anything without asking God first."

Morgan nodded in silent agreement.

"I have to share with you that the other day when Madison came over, I overheard what you two talked about."

"Mom, you listened to our conversation?"

"Yes, and I'm glad I did. She said Lori never bullied her or any of the other girls, but that's not quite true. Lori bullies the girls by controlling them. You see, she puts fear into them, so they go along with her to remain in the group. Lori is not a good friend."

"That's true. But today, Madison stood up to her. When Lori gave her a gift bag and not me, Madison handed me hers."

"Aw, that was nice of her."

"It sure was, but then Lori snagged it from me and threw it away."

"Geez. From now on, stay away from her, but smile and say hello when she's outside. Kill her with kindness. It might take her a long time to return it, but you need to be the better person. We should pray and ask for forgiveness."

"I can't forgive her! Not after what she's done to me!"

Her mom pulled her phone out and looked for her favorite scripture. "Read this scripture, and maybe you will understand why we pray and ask for forgiveness."

Morgan took her mom's phone and read the scripture to herself, *"And when you stand praying, if you hold anything against anyone, forgive them, so that your Father in heaven may forgive your sins." Mark 11:25 New International Version - Bible Gateway.*

"Wow, you got me. But it's hard to forgive someone who's hurt me so much."

"Yes, it can be very hard. But if you don't, then you will stay angry with Lori, and she won't care if you are angry with her or not. Remember, God is our vindicator."

They prayed for Lori and asked for God to bless her.

"Mom, why bless her? She doesn't deserve to be blessed."

"We ask God to bless her and melt away any bitterness she has in her heart and hopefully learn from her behavior. Show her kindness and grace. I'm not saying she is going to be kind to you right away, but don't return evil with evil. Every time you want to hate her, turn to God, and ask Him for help. Give it to Him and let Him help you with your anger. He will take care of you. Trust me—I know because I was bullied, and I, too, asked God to bless the person who bullied me. And you know what?"

Morgan shook her head no.

"We were never friends, but we were nice to each other. And that is good."

"I'm glad we talked. I feel better." Morgan let a tear roll down her cheek as she hugged her mom. She felt relief in her heart and went to bed that night knowing tomorrow would be a better day.

9

THE TRICK

It was early morning, and singing birds outside Morgan's bedroom window woke her with a smile on her face; she was refreshed and ready to start a new day. It was as if what Lori had done to her faded away while she slept. She reached for her phone on the nightstand, remembering she had turned it off before going to bed. Yawning and stretching, she turned her phone on, and several messages popped up from Madison.

"Hey, what's up?" Morgan replied.

"Are you okay?"

"Yeah, hanging in there. You?"

"I'm good."

"Good. I'm just waking up."

"Yeah, me too. Do you want to go for a bike ride later?"

"Sure, but not to the park."

"How about the cliff?"

"What's the cliff?"

"It's a cool place that overlooks the town."

"Yeah, sure."

"Okay, meet you out front around eleven."

"See ya then."

She stretched her arms over her head, then grabbing the sheets, flung them off her. Morgan swung her feet over the edge of the bed and got up to get something to eat. She was in such a good mood that she skipped into the kitchen, humming her favorite song. Her mom watched her dance around the kitchen while she took a bite of her toast and washed it down with coffee.

"Glad to see you are having a better day," she said, smiling.

"The birds are singing, and Madison and I are going for a bike ride later today."

"Where to?"

"The cliff."

"Where is the cliff?"

"Not sure, but I'm looking forward to finding out." She danced right over to her mom and took her hands, pulling her off the stool. Morgan spun her around, and they both did "The Twist" around the kitchen. Laughing, her mom said, "I have to catch my breath. Whew, I never expected that this morning."

"I'm full of spunk."

"Yes, you are. Okay, wild girl, you have fun today and be careful."

"You know it, Mom!"

"Just do me one big favor: If Lori comes near you, get away from her and text me right away."

"You got it."

"I'll be leaving around ten o'clock to meet a client at the office, and I probably won't get home until three."

"Ok."

Her mom kissed her on the top of her head, put her coffee cup in the dishwasher, and danced out of the kitchen. Morgan laughed as she twisted her own way to the cabinets to get cereal and pour a glass of orange juice. She was careful not to spill anything as she twisted her way back to the island and sat down to eat. While she ate, she texted Madison. After finishing her breakfast, she put her bowl and glass into the dishwasher and left the kitchen.

Walking down the hallway, Morgan yelled. "Hey, Mom? Where are you?"

"I'm in the laundry room. What's wrong?" she yelled back.

As Morgan hurried into the laundry room, she said, "Nothing is wrong. I'm excited that I've made a friend and will be enjoying an afternoon with her."

Holding up Morgan's grass-stained shorts, her mom said, "Ya know, this makes me angry. That little girl better watch herself around you and me. She might find it easy to bully a girl, but she might find out Mama means business if I ever hear about her hurting you again."

"Easy, Mom. Don't go crazy on me," Morgan said as she laughed at her.

She huffed, "I'm just angry, that's all."

"Okay, okay. I get your anger, but it doesn't change her."

"Why are you so smart?"

"I got my smarts from you," she said as she winked at her mom and then hugged her. Stepping backward she said, "You're the best!"

"I know. Love you."

"Love you more." She smiled at her and then ran upstairs. Morgan walked into her bedroom and, using her foot, swung the door closed and leaped onto her bed. She grabbed one of her throw pillows, tucked it under her head, and then brought her legs up to her chest and crossed them. Swinging her right foot and playing music she'd downloaded onto her phone, she started to sing along. Morgan picked up Mr. Binks the Bear and started to move him around like he was dancing. Her spirits were much better. A little while later, she heard a knock at the door.

Turning the volume down on her phone she said, "Yeah?"

Her mom opened the door. "Hey honey, I'm off to the office. I'll see you around three."

"Okay, see ya."

She laughed. "See ya, and I love you!"

"Love you, too!"

Morgan was enjoying the music so much that she forgot about the time. A text message from Madison popped up on her screen.

"Hey, where are you?"

"Oh, my gosh! I'll be with you shortly!"

She turned off the music, jumped off the bed, and then rushed down the stairs to the garage. Morgan opened the big garage door to see Madison waiting for her. She quickly put on her helmet and rode down the driveway to meet her.

"I'm sorry I'm late."

"No worries. I thought you forgot."

"I was listening to music."

"Oh. Ready?"

"Yup."

They pushed off and peddled away, heading toward the park.

Morgan grew nervous as they rode closer to the park. "I thought we were going to the cliff?"

"We are. We have to take the path past the pond."

"Oh, I never saw the path."

"It's hard to see from the swings. Whats wrong with you?" asked Madison.

"Nothing. Guess I'm looking for Lori."

"Don't worry, Lori's not home today."

"She's not?" A wave of relief washed over Morgan.

"No, she's at her grandmother's."

"Oh, okay."

"Just follow me, and everything will be okay."

The girls rode past the pond, and among the trees, a path appeared. They rode for a long time before making it to a clearing filled with blue sky, sun, and the sound of waves hitting the rocks below. Morgan didn't know Lori was hiding in the bushes waiting for the girls to arrive.

Madison said, "Let's leave the bikes and walk over to the cliff. I want you to take in the splendor of the awesome view."

"Okay. Wow, this is beautiful! Love it," Morgan said as awe and excitement came over her.

"Sure is."

"Look at the people walking around the town. They look like black dots."

"Yeah, they do."

"I'm so glad we moved here. I just love it."

Madison giggled and smiled at Morgan. "Ya know, I'm glad you moved here too."

Morgan returned her smile and sat down on the ground to enjoy the view as Madison did the same. They talked for a long time while Lori watched them, waiting for the right time. She quickly and quietly snuck from her hiding place in the woods—leaving her bike hidden under some bushes—and took Morgan's bike. She walked it away from its spot until she was out of sight and then rode away on Morgan's bike.

"Oh, my gosh! We've been talking for a long time. We probably should head back home," said Madison.

"Yeah, we should."

They got up, brushed the dirt off their clothes, and then walked over to where they left their bikes.

"My bike—it's gone! Where did it go?"

"I'm sorry, Morgan, it was Lori."

"What? Why?"

"She had me bring you here so she could take your bike."

Morgan was devastated. "I thought we were becoming friends. How could you hurt me like this?"

Madison looked at her but couldn't say anything. Her heart sank in her chest as she climbed on her bike and rode off. It pained her to leave Morgan behind, but Lori had threatened her, and she was afraid. Morgan watched Madison ride away and started to cry as she pulled her phone from her back pocket to text her mom.

Her frustration grew worse as she yelled, "No service. Seriously? Dang! I don't believe it. The *one* time I need my phone the most." Morgan walked around holding her phone up but got nothing. She was disappointed in Madison but also in herself for trusting her. She had a long walk ahead, but she knew she could and would make it by herself. While following the path, she would keep trying to text her mom.

When Mrs. Jones arrived home early, she noticed the garage door was open. She remembered closing it when she left, so she entered the house calling for Morgan but got no answer. Her mom hated when Morgan left the garage door open when no one was home.

As she walked past the window, she looked outside just as Madison rode by on her bike—alone. She thought that was strange because they were supposed to ride their bikes together. Half an hour went by, and still Morgan was not home; her mom started to panic.

"Where could she be?" She went outside and looked up and down the road but couldn't find Morgan.

"Mrs. Jones," Madison said as she ran outside to catch Morgan's mom.

"Hi, Madison. Is Morgan with you?"

"No. She's not. I have something to tell you but not out here."

"Well, okay. Let's go inside." As they walked back to Morgan's house, Madison turned her head and saw Lori watching from her bedroom window.

"Come in the kitchen, Madison."

They sat down at the island, and Madison said, "I've been nervously pacing my bedroom floor because of what happened today at the cliff."

"Where is she?"

"Please promise not to tell my mom."

"I can't promise that Madison. It will depend on what this is about."

"Can we take your car to the park?"

"What now? Oh, God! Is she hurt?"

"I don't know. Please, can we go?" They hurried out the front door to the car. On the ride to the park, Madison said, "We went to the cliff. Lori wanted me to take Morgan to the cliff, and I did."

"Did Lori hurt her?"

"No, she took her bike, and I rode away leaving her stranded without a bike."

"Why?"

Madison started crying, "I'm afraid of Lori."

Morgan's mom tried to comfort her. She put her hand on the girl's shoulder and said, "I understand how frightened you are of Lori, but leaving my daughter alone at the cliff was a bad idea."

"I know it was, and I'm very sorry."

They arrived at the park and got out with Madison leading the way to the path. As they walked, they called Morgan's name. Finally, in the distance, they heard her respond.

"I'm here! I'm here!"

They ran toward her voice, and when Morgan saw her mom, she ran to her. They held each other for a long time.

"Are you okay?" her mom asked.

"I'm thirsty and tired, but okay." Morgan looked angrily at Madison. "Why is she here?"

"She told me what happened. She wanted to help find you."

Madison stepped forward with fresh tears in her eyes. "Morgan, I'm sorry. Please believe me; I'm deeply sorry."

"It seems to me you're always sorry, and I'm always trusting you. I just can't trust you anymore," Morgan said.

"I don't blame you if you never trust me again."

"Why should I?"

Morgan's mom moved between them. "Girls, girls, stop. This is not helping the situation. We're here, and you're okay. So, let's go home."

Everyone was quiet on the walk back to the car. As Mrs. Jones drove, she addressed Madison. "I hope you have learned a lesson."

"I sure have."

At home, Morgan got out of the car, refusing to look at Madison. She tried to walk past her, but Madison stepped in front of her. Again, Morgan tried to walk around, but Madison put her hand up to stop her and said, "Hear me out, please."

"Why should I?"

"I get it. You're mad at me and have every right to be. Just hear me out."

Morgan crossed her arms and spoke harshly. "Fine."

"Lori threatened me. I should never have done what I did. I'm truly sorry, and I will never hurt you again. That's a promise."

Morgan took a deep breath and let it out slowly, "Don't promise something you can't keep."

"You have my word. I'm done with her."

Morgan's mom interrupted. "We have to figure out how to deal with Lori and stop her from bullying the two of you."

"Me? You think she is bullying me?" said Madison.

"Yes, I do. She uses her control to manipulate you into doing things you don't want to do. She puts fear into you. That is bullying."

"I never thought of it that way."

"She's playing both of you, and I don't like it. Madison, does your mom know where you are?"

"No. I'll text her and let her know I'm here."

"Ask her if she can come over to our house."

After a few minutes, Madison's phone dinged in response. "My mom will be over in a few minutes."

"Perfect."

When Madison's mom arrived, they greeted each other and sat at the kitchen table. Mrs. Jones explained what happened to Morgan. Then, Mrs. Roberts shared how Lori has been disrespectful to her daughter and felt it was time to put a stop to it before it gets out of control. While the moms drank coffee and the girls had chocolate chip cookies with milk, they concluded they needed to talk with both Lori and her mom.

10

THE CONFRONTATION

"I think we just have to come out and tell her what Lori has been doing to the girls," said Madison's mom. "I wonder how she'll handle it."

"I've known her for a while, and we get together on occasion to talk and have a glass of wine. I think she'll be more open to me starting the conversation, even though it was Morgan's bike that was taken. I told Lori to invite Morgan to her birthday party and to be kind to her. I feel responsible for some of this mess," Mrs. Roberts said.

"No, don't feel that way. You had no idea what she was capable of doing."

"Maybe so, but as I said, I've watched her behavior with Madison. I'll text Mrs. Fletcher now and find out if she is home and explain that we want to visit with her."

They waited anxiously for Lori's mom to respond to the text. "A text is coming in from her. We can come over."

"Perfect. Okay, *Mission Lori* is about to start." They clapped their hands together and high-fived as they got up from the table to leave.

Everyone put on their shoes and walked to Lori's house.

Mrs. Jones let out a deep breath as they approached, "I'm so nervous."

"Uh-huh. Me too." Mrs. Roberts said with trepidation in her voice.

As Madison's mom pushed the doorbell, she said, "Here goes nothing."

Mrs. Fletcher answered the door. "Oh, my, I didn't expect such a group of people. Please, please come in."

They all stepped inside, and Lori rushed down the stairs and into the foyer to stand next to her mom. She gave her daughter a strange look. "Shall we go to the porch to sit down?"

"Yes, that would be lovely," Mrs. Roberts said.

"Can I get anyone a drink? Water?"

"No, thank you. We have something to discuss with you, and I know it will be hard to hear. But it must be said."

Before she could continue, Morgan's mom jumped to the chase, "Lori has been bullying my daughter and took her bike today when she and Madison were at the cliff."

"I don't know you very well, but that can't be true. My daughter would never do that."

"It's true," Madison said.

"They're lying. I didn't take her stupid bike!" Lori yelled.

Mrs. Fletcher looked at her, and she stopped her daughter from talking with a movement of her hand before turning back to Morgan's mom. "Please continue."

"You see, the bullying has been going on for some time now. She bullied her at the park, at her birthday party, and now at the cliff."

"Not all of that is true. I was at the birthday party, and I didn't see Lori bullying your daughter."

Madison spoke up again. "Every time you left the party, that's when she was mean to her."

"Liar!"

"Lori, stop saying that. Tell me the truth. Did you take her bike, and have you been bullying her?"

"I don't have her bike. No. I'm not bullying her!"

Mrs. Fletcher turned back to the other moms.

"Why is she so upset if she's not doing anything wrong? If Lori doesn't have her bike, then you wouldn't mind if we look in your garage?" Mrs. Jones asked.

"No, I don't mind if we check my garage if it stops the false accusations."

"I can explain everything, Mom. I just borrowed her bike today, right, Morgan?" Lori looked at Morgan, an unspoken threat in her eyes.

"I don't understand, Lori. You said you didn't have my daughter's bike before, but now you are saying you borrowed it?"

"And trying to get Morgan to agree with you?" Mrs. Roberts added.

"What's going on, Lori?" her mom asked.

Morgan finally spoke up, "She tricked Madison and me into riding our bikes to the cliff today and then stole my bike, leaving me stranded. I had to walk all the way back by myself until my mom and Madison found me."

"That doesn't make any sense. Why would Madison leave you behind if my daughter was the one who tricked you?" She looked at Lori, who had flopped on the sofa and crossed her arms.

"I can explain," Madison said. "Lori called me yesterday and told me to take Morgan to the cliff. She said if I didn't, she would make my life miserable, so I was afraid and went along with it. But when I saw Mrs. Jones outside, I knew I had to say something, or at least find out what she was doing. She told me she was concerned about Morgan. So, we went inside, and I told her we needed to go to the park. During the car ride, I told her what happened. Then we went after Morgan. That's the truth."

"All of that is true," Mrs. Jones confirmed.

Lori was still sitting across from the girls, and she had a look to kill in her eyes; Morgan shuffled nervously.

"I just can't believe Lori would do such a thing. Although, you *are* acting funny," she said, looking at her daughter. "Let's go to the garage and see if Morgan's bike is there."

Lori was nervous as they left the porch, and she moped all the way through the house. She knew she was busted, and it was the end of the line for her.

Mrs. Fletcher opened the door and went into the garage; everyone except Lori crowded into the doorway. Morgan's bike leaned against the wall near the big overhead door.

"Oh, dear! Morgan, I'm so sorry. Lori, where is your bike?"

Everyone turned toward the girl and moved out of her way. Lori sulked with head down while walking toward her mom, "It's at the cliff, hidden in the woods."

"What? Lori, why did you take Morgan's bike? Tell me right now!"

Tears streamed as all the pent-up feelings poured out in her words. "Because I hate her! She moved into Katie's house, and Katie and I were good friends. Morgan took her place, and I don't like it. I hate Morgan for moving into her house."

"It's no longer Katie's house, Lori. It belongs to the Joneses now. You can't just take people's personal items—it's so wrong. I'm sorry this happened, Morgan."

Madison spoke up, "It's not just Morgan she bullies. She bullies me, too, by making me do things to hurt Morgan."

"That's true," Mrs. Roberts said. "A couple of nights ago, Lori came to our house and was very disrespectful to Madison."

"This behavior is unacceptable, Lori. I'm so embarrassed. We will talk about this later."

Mrs. Fletcher went to Morgan as she wiped her tears from her face. "Morgan, I'm sorry for what you have gone through. I feel terrible about this. Her father and I split several months ago—we were fighting a lot—and it upset Lori. Her father and I started talking again recently and realized we love each other very much and want to make it work. Our careers got in the way of family and our relationship, but that's all going to change."

She looked at Lori. "He's moving back home this weekend."

Lori looked up at her mom with joy in her eyes. "He is? Really?"

"Yes, he really is." She hugged her daughter and then lifted her chin to look into her eyes. "This doesn't mean you are not going to be punished for your behavior."

Lori looked down at the floor, "Yes, Mom. I understand. Can I go to my room?"

"Go ahead."

The girl refused to look at anyone as she raced past them and up the stairs.

"I hope things get better for you and your family. I'm sorry for what you have been going through. It must be so hard for all of you," Mrs. Jones said.

"It hasn't been easy. Lori visits her grandmother on the weekends and spends time with her father. It was his mother who showed us how to make things better."

Mrs. Jones gave her a hug and then grabbed her hands and said, "We don't know each other very well yet, but I'm here for you."

"Thank you for listening," said Mrs. Fletcher as she looked at Mrs. Jones with kind eyes.

Mrs. Fletcher turned to Morgan again. "I apologize for Lori's behavior and promise she will never hurt you again. If she does, come to me right away, and I will stop her. I hope she gets better as we become a family again."

"Mrs. Fletcher, I understand now why she was hurting me, even though it wasn't right. I will pray for her."

Lori's mom hugged Morgan, and it turned into a group hug. Everyone said goodbye to Lori's mom and walked back over to the Joneses' house while Morgan rode her bike out of the garage and across the street.

11

JOURNEY'S END

They stood in the foyer looking at each other with big smiles on their faces and then let out a huge breath of relief. Laughing, Madison said, "I'm glad that's over."

"Me too," Morgan agreed.

Mrs. Jones sat on the bench. "It went better than I thought."

"It sure did," said Madison's mom.

"I'm glad it's over. I feel bad for Lori. I hope she learns a lesson from this. Mom, when you said to pray for her and to bless her, I'm glad we did," Morgan said.

"Oh, honey, it's so true. We never know what people are going through. That's why it's important to be kind even if they are being mean."

"I hope things get better for all of them. People getting hurt can cause them to hurt others," Mrs. Roberts said.

The girls nodded in agreement.

"I know one thing: I hope we can be friends, Morgan."

"I'm all for that."

Morgan's mom stood and clapped her hands. "Well, this is a cause for celebration! How about dinner at the Hungry Seagull?"

"I'm in," said Madison.

"Me too!" said Mrs. Roberts with a smile on her face.

Mrs. Jones said, "We can take my car."

The moms put their arms around each other's waist and squeezed a little side hug when they got to the car, and the giggling girls got into the back seat. New friendships started on that drive to the restaurant.

The girls never became friends with Lori. She had broken their trust. But every time they saw her, they were nice to her. Morgan and Madison became inseparable; they hung out together at each other's house or at the beach, playing volleyball with some girls from town.

Lori's family got back together. Things got better for her, although she learned a hard lesson and had to talk with her priest about what she was going through. She remained friends with a couple of other girls in the neighborhood, but two other girls were not allowed to play with her after their parents heard about what she did to Morgan.

Bullies never win in the end. Sometimes they not only lose friends but also damage their reputation. Remember, always seek someone to talk to about bullying, Mrs. Roberts said. If you are a victim of bullying, learn how to protect yourself and seek help from an adult, teacher, priest, reverend, or friend.

DISCUSSION QUESTIONS

1. Have you ever been a victim of bullying? How did it make you feel?
2. What do you think is the takeaway from the story?
3. How did someone help you deal with bullying?
4. How did the scripture in the story help you deal with forgiveness?

ABOUT THE AUTHOR

Molly Johnston has struggled with finding her place in the world for a long time. As a child and woman, she struggled with being bullied and was never part of a group of friends. As a result, she became a loner and introvert from an incredibly young age. Her faith has helped her to develop into a bright, confident, and loving person and has given her strength to fight against bullying. Today, Molly  is a leader with a soul filled with compassion and kindness. Being bullied didn't break her down. It taught her to fight for what is right and pushed her to fulfill her dreams of becoming a leader and entrepreneur.

Made in the USA
Middletown, DE
28 June 2022

67718427R00040